Augustus Semonnier

The Recognition

A drama of the Fifteenth Century

Augustus Semonnier

The Recognition
A drama of the Fifteenth Century

ISBN/EAN: 9783337343699

Printed in Europe, USA, Canada, Australia, Japan

Cover: Foto ©Andreas Hilbeck / pixelio.de

More available books at **www.hansebooks.com**

THE RECOGNITION.

A DRAMA OF THE FIFTEENTH CENTURY,

(For Male Characters Only.)

By A. L.

WITH STAGE DIRECTIONS,

Cast of Characters, Relative Positions, Costumes, Synopsis of Scenes, etc.

EDITED AND PUBLISHED BY

Joseph A. Lyons, A. M.

NOTRE DAME, INDIANA:
UNIVERSITY PRESS.
1885.

PREFACE.

THE plot of the play is simple, as it turns on the recognition of a son after several years' separation from his father. The scene is laid in Italy, in the fifteenth century. The Duke of Spoleto, indulging in one of those feuds which seem to have been the greatest luxury of the "bold old barons" of the time, had an idea of waging war against the Prince of Macerata, who, in case of the death of the duke's son, would be the legal heir to the duke's possessions.

The first scene of Act First opens immediately after a battle between the troops of the prince and those of the duke. The duke loses the battle and his son. To prevent the prince from becoming his heir, he reports that his son was only wounded, and seizes Antonio, the son of Count Bartolo, conveys him to one of his castles, persuades the boy that Count Bartolo, his father, knows where he is, and in course of time tells Antonio that the count is dead, and that he (Antonio) shall be henceforth his son and heir, and adopt the name of Julio. Count Bartolo all this while is searching after Antonio, and, convinced that he is in the hands of the duke, takes sides with the Prince of Macerata.

The chances of war go against the prince ; he is forced to retire to the city of Macerata, is then killed, and Bartolo succeeds him in command. In the meantime, Antonio is taken prisoner by Bartolo's men, and cast into prison without being seen by Bartolo, who supposes the captive boy to be the duke's son. Hoping to check the duke, Bartolo sends him word to retire from the siege of Macerata, or that his son will be put to death. The duke, instead of withdrawing, presses the siege more eagerly, thinking he can take the city and secure Bartolo before the injured father can see his captive son.

But Bartolo sends for Antonio, whom he takes to be Julio,

the duke's son, and, of course, when he appears, is at once recognized by his father and all present. At this time, the duke rushes in with his soldiers, attempts to seize Antonio, is frustrated in his design, receives a death-blow, and dies, begging pardon of Bartolo for the injury he has inflicted upon him.

This simple little story has been exceedingly well brought out in the various scenes.

Dramatis Personæ.

DUKE OF SPOLETO.

RICCARDO, his Squire.

PRINCE OF MACERATA.

COUNT BARTOLO.

ANTONIO, his Son, a Boy.

BALTHAZAR (Arbalester), Friend of Antonio.

STEPHANO, Teacher of Antonio.

LEONARDO, a Soldier.

GRATIANO,
LORENZO, } Pages, Friends of Antonio.

GIACOMO, Squire to Bartolo.

FABIANO, Governor of Montefalco.

REGINALD, Officer of the Prince of Macerata.

PAOLO, a Jailer.

ZUCCHI, a Blacksmith.

ANDREA, a Squire of the Duke.

MARSO, a Soldier.

PIETRO,
BEPPO,
PACIFICO, } Attendants of Bartolo.
ALPHONSO,

ORLANDO, Officer of the Prince.

ALBERTO,
GABRINI,
CASTELLO, } Citizens.
ORAZZI,

SILVIO, a Courier.

CARLO,
ALFIERI, } Soldiers of the Duke.
ALMENO,

RAFAELE,
MANFRED, } Officers of the Prince's Guard.
ANGELO,

GUARDS, etc.

COSTUMES.

DUKE OF SPOLETO: *First Costume.*—Dark cloak, riding boots. Dark hat and crimson plumes. *Act III, Scene I:* Crimson and gold doublet, short cloak and trunk hose, cap and feather, pink silk stockings, shoes with diamond buckles. *Scene III:* Ducal coronet and robes.

RICCARDO: *First costume.*—Dark cloak, etc., like the Duke. *Second costume:* Doublet, short cloak trunks, cap and feather, dark brown and amber.

PRINCE OF MACERATA. — Short cloak, doublet, trunks, cap and feather, etc., in purple and white.

COUNT BARTOLO.—Same costume in maroon and violet.

ANTONIO: *First costume.*—Boy's tunic and leggins—white, with blue scarf. Cap and feather. *Second costume:* Short cloak, doublet, trunks cap and feather, purple and gold.

BALTHAZAR.—Buff coat, and armor of the period.

STEPHANO.—University cap and gown—black.

LEONARDO, *and the other soldiers of the* DUKE.—Buff coats, and armor of the period, with red facings and badges.

ORLANDO, *and officers of the* PRINCE'S *guard.*—Same, with blue facings and badges.

ATTENDANTS OF BARTOLO.—Same, with yellow facings and badges.

LORENZO.—Same as ANTONIO's *second costume,* but in green and pink.

GRATIANO.—Same as ANTONIO's *second costume,* but in blue and silver.

GIACOMO.—Short cloak, doublet, trunks, cap and feather in dark green and gold.

FABIANO.—Short cloak, doublet, trunks, cap and feather in scarlet and white.

REGINALD.—Short cloak, doublet, trunks, cap and feather in dark blue and amber.

PAOLO.—Buff coat and armor of the period.

ZUCCHI.—Grey doublet and hose. Black skull cap. Blacksmith's leather apron.

ANDREA.—Short cloak, doublet, trunks, cap and feather—in crimson and gold.

MARSO.—Buff coat and armor of the period.

SILVIO.—Tunic and leggins. Cap and feather—light green and silver.

CITIZENS.—Doublet and hose—parti-colored.

Synopsis of Scenes.

———O———

ACT FOURTH — Scene First.

The Besieged town—The Chieftain's Prayer—Bartolo's Address to the
Soldiers and Citizens—Sad news of the Prince's Death
— Capture of Julio.

Scene Second.

Scene in the Prison—Balthazar Caught.

Scene Third.

Tent of the Duke—Frustrated Hopes.

Scene Fourth.

Last Address of Bartolo —The Prisoners are brought before him—THE
RECOGNITION of Antonio by Bartolo—Balthazar kills the
Duke, who is forgiven by Bartolo and Antonio.

STAGE DIRECTIONS.

(The reader is supposed to be on the stage, facing the audience.)

EXITS AND ENTRANCES.

R. means *Right;* L., *Left;* R. D., *Right Door;* L. D., *Left Door;*
S. E., *Second Entrance;* U. E., *Upper Entrance;* M. D., *Middle Door.*

RELATIVE POSITIONS.

R. means *Right;* L., *Left;* C., *Centre;* R. C., *Right of Centre;* L. C.,
Left of Centre.

Prologue.

Our play, "The Recognition," has been laid
In olden times, when men fought blade to blade;
They wore strong armor, cast in shining steel,
Protecting all the form from head to heel.
With breast-plate, gauntlets, and strong coat-of-mail,
Visor and helmet plumed with feathers pale:
In fact, so different were the customs then,
They must have seemed another race of men.
Or, may be not. No matter! In our play
We find a Duke, whose son was killed one day;
And by that death the Duke's estate will go
To fill the coffers of his deadly foe,
Macerata's Prince. This adds to his great grief;
"How can I," cries he, "hide this from the chief?"

We mark now wherefore he would fain avoid
To let him know his son's life was destroyed;
How, later, he was tempted to decoy,
To kidnap, and to claim another boy,
Antonio by name. His face is fair,
And strong resemblance to the dead doth bear.
He meets the Duke in an unguarded hour;
The young Antonio falls within his power.
Time rolls away. The Duke, to seal his plot,
Tells the poor youth his father, loved, lives not.

As Julio known, heir to his large estates,
The stolen boy in ducal castle waits;
Meanwhile, the injured father joins the fight,
Defending 'gainst Duke Macerata's right.

The Prince at last is slain. Now in command,
Antonio's father rules Macerata's band.
The boy, the Duke's hope, is a prisoner made,
His jailers little dreaming that, betrayed
By the fierce Duke, the slender, gentle youth
Is their commander's son in very truth.

The injured father, sure that fettered fast
He holds the foeman's only son at last,
Bids him retire: else, threatens to destroy
The prisoner's life, that of the gentle boy.

The Duke heeds not, but presses in hot haste
Before the thread of his dark plot be traced;
Before the father shall have met the son:
Determined his bold purpose shall be won.

The youthful prisoner, summoned, stands amazed;
Has his dear father from the dead been raised?
They recognize each other, they embrace
Just as the baffled duke has reached the place
To meet his death-blow, for the *truth is known.*

Antonio, now an heir to ducal throne,
Restored to friends and home, thanks from his heart
The Blessed Virgin that she took his part.

The Recognition.

ACT FIRST.

SCENE I.

Night—The mountain pass—Wild scenery—To right foreground of stage a huge rock projects, at left back a narrow pass ascending from right centre to left, and thence across the flat. Duke of Spoleto and his companion, RICCARDO, making their way stealthily from behind the rock. (R.)

RICCARDO. My lord duke, I think this is the way. (*He points out to the pass, L..*)

DUKE. Are you sure your memory does not fail you? In this dark night even the chamois could not find his path.

RICC. Yonder is the steep ascent. (*Hearing some noise, L.*) Do you hear that noise? Some one above is stirring.

DUKE. Stay! stay! Riccardo!—an enemy might lurk in these crags; prepare your bow and be ready.

RICC. Shall I shoot in the dark?

DUKE. Listen, I pray, and be on your guard; one false shot might expose us and draw the foe on our track. Better retreat to this obscure recess, and wait for what may come. (*They retreat to the cavity in the rocks, R. 2 E. their eyes constantly fixed on one spot.*)

RICC. My lord, I shall guard this narrow defile; one man here is as good as an army, and should a Maceratan show his armor, I—

DUKE. (*Interrupting.*) Riccardo, if there is a time when bravery is out of place, it is now; spare your arrows and listen. (*They listen. Steps are heard up in the pass, L.*)

RICC. I distinctly hear footsteps; some one is coming. He stops. It is no soldier—it is the light step of a mountaineer.

DUKE. (*Listening an instant.*) He must have overheard you, for he has stopped suddenly. Let him pass; disturb him not; no doubt he is some hunter returning to his cot, perhaps bearing his prey, and feeling his way in the dark. Do not show yourself nor discover your colors. In these days every man is, at once, friend and enemy. Withdraw to this cavity in the rock. Tell me, Riccardo, of the sad event which to-day has brought ruin and death to my house and to me. (*They withdraw to the cavity in front of the projecting rock*, R.I.E.)

RICC. My lord, it is too painful to recall.

DUKE. Painful to me above all, Riccardo, yet will you refuse me this consolation in my bereavement? Where was Julio killed?

RICC. Just at the door of my tent, lord duke. I bade him seek safety there, and reluctantly he retraced his steps from the field, when an arrow overtook him—an arrow aimed by a cruel hand!

DUKE. Was the shaft aimed at the boy? Did the enemy guess it was my son? Did he fall?

RICC. I saw him entering his tent, his hand grasping the weapon that had pierced him; there I lost sight of him. When I returned to the tent he had breathed his last. Orlando and I wrapped him in a cloak and carried him away.

DUKE. O Riccardo! Riccardo! it was little to lose the battle, but to lose my Julio—my beloved boy, my hope!—and to think that the Maceratan claims my estate—to think that he is my legal heir,—it is too much for the heart of a proud knight, and of a father!

RICC. It is sad, my lord, sad to have lost him—worse than ten thousand defeats.

DUKE. (*Sighing with emotion.*) Where did you leave the body?

RICC. In the middle of the night we buried the remains, my lord, and placed a stone to mark the spot. The grave is under the large olive trees on the other side of the mountain. Are you satisfied that no one should have witnessed the sad ceremony?

DUKE. I am, Riccardo. The news of Julio's death would have given more joy to the base hearts of our enemy than the capture of Spoleto itself. I wish it be a secret to all till more propitious days shall dawn upon us; but hark! (*The sound of steps above*, L.)

RICC. It is the same step approaching. My lord, shall I go forth?

DUKE. Stay—listen! (*A beautiful song is heard*, L.) What a clear, beautiful voice! It sounds like that of Julio; hear what he says. He is a boy—no doubt a mountaineer. Oh! such a brave boy clambering those rugged rocks must be a noble lad. Where are you going, Riccardo?

(RICCARDO *goes out of the recess, the boy jumps from the rock, C. and finds himself in the presence of* RICCARDO; *both view each other in amazement;* RICCARDO *is about to shoot.*)

DUKE. (*Coming to the boy, C.*) Hold, Riccardo!

ANTONIO. Oh, pity! Do not kill me, pray!

DUKE. Be not afraid, my lad; your charming voice attracted us, and we wondered that in such a dangerous spot anyone could be found at this hour of the night. Why did you sing?

ANT. Sir, I remained longer than usual in the mountains; the deer absorbed my attention so that I forgot the lateness of the hour, and nearly lost my path. I sing at times, when I am alone and afraid; I thought I heard some one speaking, and to calm my fears I sang.

DUKE. Is there anyone here of whom you might be afraid?

ANT. So far as I know, you and your companion are kind and of good birth; may I ask your name?

DUKE. I have the right to ask yours first, child.

ANT. Antonio, sir, is my name.

DUKE. It is a beautiful one; it is also that of your father, no doubt.

ANT. No, sir; my father's name is Count Bartolo, whose castle you may have seen yonder on the mountain. He is now awaiting me; would you desire to pass the night under our roof?

DUKE. There are reasons to urge me on now; our army is moving, and, to meet it, I must go through this rocky path. Riccardo, how remarkably like Julio this boy is!

RICC. He could play his part well and serve your designs, my lord.

DUKE. (*Aside to* RICCARDO.) Riccardo, this amazes me; could not this boy be my Julio, restored to a new life? Do you not believe that such a thing could be?

RICC. Dream not, my lord, nor let your reason be confused

by false imaginations. This lad is like Julio in form; his voice has the same mellow accents, but his age, my lord, his age—he is younger by some years.

DUKE. Enough, Riccardo. I am resolved to try even this unjust policy to save my name. (*To* ANTONIO.) Boy, the name of your father is familiar to me. Why, Riccardo, it was Bartolo at whose castle we rested but a few hours ago; it was he who led us down the steep road, and marked out our path through these defiles.

ANT. My father—do you know him? Was he anxious about me?

DUKE. It was three hours ago, and he showed no anxiety about your delay, beyond the meaning that his last words conveyed. "My son," said he, "is now in the mountains; should you meet him, Antonio is fearless and sure; bid him, in my name, to direct you, and even accompany you as far as you desire."

RICC. He uttered those words; I remember them distinctly. (*Aside.*) I may just as well confirm the assertion of the duke. I see his aim, although I hate a lie.

ANT. Well, my lords, you may command me in my father's name; pray, tell me your own, that I may remember his friends.

DUKE. The Duke of Spoleto is my glorious name, child.

ANT. (*Withdrawing* L. *aside.*) Never heard it mentioned in a friendly manner in the halls of my father.

DUKE. And in my companion behold the first knight of my dukedom, Riccardo of Otranto.

ANT. (*Aside.*) Still more obscure to me. (*Aloud.*) My age and my little acquaintance beyond these mountains will excuse my not knowing you, my lords; you are the friends of my father: I will accompany you, even as far as Spoleto.

DUKE. Once there, we will send a message to your honored father.

RICC. It is a cruel theft, which no gold can repair; such a fine youth!

DUKE. This is the way up the mountain (*pointing out*, c.) is it?

ANT. Yes; let me go first, please your Excellency.

RICC. I see lights below; some one is on our track. (*All look.. L.U.E.*) Boy, there are brigands in these places.

ANT. We will soon be out of their reach; come, follow me.

RICC. These men are the soldiers of the prince. May we avoid them! (*They ascend the mountain rocks and disappear.* R.U.E. *Music.*)

SCENE II.

Enter (L.U.E.) on the Stage, from behind the projecting rock of foreground, old COUNT BARTOLO, GIACOMO, his squire, four or five attendants, all of whom carry torches and seem absorbed, searching hither and thither.

BARTOLO. Gently, my faithful attendants; search diligently. Do not tread upon him; he may be asleep.

ALL THE ATTENDANTS. No doubt, my lord, sleep has overtaken him somewhere about here.

GIACOMO. (*To* ATTENDANTS.) Do the bidding of our lord. (*Aside.*) He may have fallen in a pit. Merciful God, save him from danger!

BART. (*Comes in front of the rock.*) Here, perhaps, in this recess; bring your torches. (*They find an arrow.*) An arrow here! Some one has passed here, then. (*They crowd upon each other to look at the arrow.*)

GIAC. Hunters, my lord, frequent these passes, and no doubt this arrow was dropped; it was not used. (*Looking at it.*)

PIETRO. My lord, I shall climb to the rocks above; I know the path well; there is a cliff which only agile feet can ascend. Perhaps he has fallen in the dark.

BEPPO *and* PACIFICO. We also shall go with him. This is a sad adventure.

BART. Spare no pains, good men; search every nook and crevice. Whoever brings my Antonio shall receive his ample reward.

GIAC. Poor Antonio! his absence sorely is felt. The halls of the castle are deserted; mirth is gone, and we are on these cliffs instead of in our peaceful couches.

PIETRO. (*From the rocks above.*) My lord, his scarf! the blue scarf his mother gave him—the blue-colored sash of the Virgin!—He has left it here.

BART. His sash, do you say? Bring it to me. Is that all you can discover?

BEPPO. It is so dark we cannot see.

PACIFICO. Search is vain before the dawn of day shall penetrate these dark places. (*They continue searching. The* 1ST ATTEND., *having come down, brings the scarf to the old man, who, pressing it to his heart and lips, exclaims:*)

BART. Blessed memento! how dear to me! How you grieve me! Sad token of my absent son!

GIAC. My lord, it is not torn; it was unlaced by his own gentle hand; on it no mark of violence is visible. Perhaps it prevented his progress, or endangered his steps.

BART. No doubt you are right; in vain I vex myself: my son may have already returned to the castle by another way.

PIETRO. My lord, all further search is unavailing in the dark. I may grieve you, perhaps, if I say there is no other way than this to the castle, and therefore it would be foolish to fancy that Antonio, our young master, has returned.

BART. We shall come again to-morrow, when the light of day shall encircle these wild mountains. We will now go home.

GIAC. My lord, we would expose our lives in the attempt. We cannot go back before the daylight. Rest here on this fallen trunk of a tree, and try to forget your sorrow in quiet sleep.

BART. Be it as you say, Giacomo. (*Goes to the log*, R. *assisted by* GIACOMO, *sits.*) Fatigue overpowers me! Alas! may God save my Antonio, and preserve him to his father! (*The* ATTENDANTS *draw around silently to look at the old man.*)

ATTEND. How sad it is to see him so exhausted! Our dear old master! (*They continue looking on.*)

GIAC. Put out the fires, men, and go to rest. (ATTEND-ANTS *extinguish their torches, and together sing, softly.*)

All the ATTENDANTS *sing:*

> Break not his soothing slumbers,
> His soul is charged with grief:
> Fresh woe his heart encumbers,
> Sleep brings him fond relief.

Duet. Perhaps he now is dreaming
> Of his noble, darling boy,
> His eye with bliss is beaming,
> Let not a sound destroy

Chorus. The short but sweet delusion,
> The respite he is taking
> From sorrow's cold intrusion,
> That waits his sad awaking.

(*They fall asleep, and silence reigns.*)

BART. (*Reclining on the shoulder of* GIACOMO, *dreams, and talks in his sleep.*) Antonio, beware—beware the pit! Ah! Antonio, come back! What, you would take him away? Stop, men! stop! Antonio, escape! (*Wakes, haggard and terrified.*) Giacomo, is that you? Oh! I had a horrible dream! I beheld Antonio taken away by the troops of the Spoletan. (*Rises.*) It is possible.

GIAC. Nay, my lord, more than possible; it explains all. Fearless as he is, Antonio would now be at home had no one intercepted him. (*Enter the* PRINCE OF MACERATA, L. 2 E. *with a long suite of lords and attendants, the latter bearing torches. The attendants come in first, and look distrustfully on* BARTOLO *and his men.*)

1ST OFF., REGINALD. (L.) (*Shouts the password.*) Macerata forever!

ATTENDANTS OF BARTOLO. (R.) Macerata forever! We are friends.

PRINCE. (L.) Who are these men? What are they doing, lingering about these passes?

GIAC. (R.) Lord prince, listen to my words. We owe to a sad accident our presence in these deserted regions. Our noble count, Bartolo, whom you behold, has lost his son, and in search of him we came with the purpose of ascertaining the fate of the boy; but we have as yet no clue. Here is the only indication of his having passed this way. (*Shows the scarf.*)

PRINCE. Count Bartolo, I sympathize with you in your affliction; your loss grieves me, because it must grieve any father, and my sympathy is all the stronger since you have ever been a staunch friend and supporter of my house. My men shall search every recess where your son might be concealed; and whether dead or alive, if he is on these mountains, they shall bring him to you.

BART. Thank you, benevolent prince. I know what you would readily do for me were my Antonio on these mountains, but in my judgment he is not; he has been kidnapped.

GIAC. The Spoletans, my prince, fled through these mountain-passes. They need men or they need vengeance, and they would not shrink from the murder of a child.

REGINALD. Your implied conjectures are very probable, noble prince.

PRINCE. (*Stopping to consider a moment.*) Yes, you are right. Even if no trace could be found which would mark the boy's passage, except this scarf, it is evident that he has been through these defiles, and my escort has not met him below. I can see no other way of explaining this sad event except that your son, noble count, has been stolen away by the banditti of the Spoletan.

BART. (*Animated.*) I would rather see him dead than subject to such a servitude! and for me, old as I am, I will gird myself for battle, and for the deliverance of my Antonio. Woe to his betrayers! God knows my distress, He sees how crushed my heart is, but vengeance now nerves my arm!

PRINCE. I will undertake your cause, worthy count. With all my heart I will come to your assistance; follow me with your men, and success shall surely crown our efforts.

BART. Rely on me and my attendants; my troops are at your command; to-morrow fifty spears shall be added to yours, and as many footmen shall side with your braves. Once more my old armor shall gleam out on the field of battle, and the cry of my youth shall urge my men to the combat (*shake hands*) to-morrow. To-morrow I shall join your standard. Adieu, all—adieu.

ALL. To-morrow! Macerata forever! (*They depart, the Maceratans going up the pass, and* BARTOLO, *with his attendants, leave by the side at which they entered.* (L.U.E.) *Orchestra plays while they dissappear.*)

ACT SECOND.

SCENE I.

A handsome apartment in the fortress of Montefalco—ANTONIO (c.) alone, dressed in rich garments— Books on a table—He stands up, looking at an arrow which he tries on a bow.

ANTONIO (*now called* JULIO). My arm is quite enfeebled by its long rest. My hand seems unskilled as when I first began to shoot at the target in my father's hall. Once I could pierce the swift chamois; strength and skill were mine; but now, I confess, I am ashamed. Old Stephano is the first cause of it. Why, if I follow his advice, I shall do nothing but study, nothing but recite. It is no fun to have him beat

me when I miss my lessons. He will come along with five
or six books, then look at me above his glasses. I guess he
means to scare me first, so that he may conquer me afterward.
Then he will put me such questions as I never dreamt of before. Dear! what have I to do with the Babylonians? They
are dead long ago, and nothing to me. Stephano thinks that
everybody is born to read books; well, I am not, surely. Here
is my duty for to-day. Ah! no, it is my father's last letter.
(*Kisses it.*) My dear father, it is little to know that you are
well only by your messages, but the duke has informed me
that my father will soon be here; the letter alludes to it, does
it not? Let me see. (*Reads.*) "Dear Antonio "—or, rather,
" Dearest Julio." (*Stops.*) Why did my father change my
name, I wonder? Antonio was his pet name, because my
mother's name was Antonia; but perhaps, as I am older, he
thought that Julio would be more befitting. "'Tis the name
of an emperor," says Stephano, and he insists that Antonio
is only a poor fisherman's name. Now this is not true; there
was an emperor of that name: I read that in his big books.
But let me read; yes, here it is: "Be of good cheer and study
well; fit yourself for the high rank which God calls on you
to occupy. I will soon judge of your progress; in the meantime I leave you under the care of God and the kind protection of our good duke." Well, well, this means what I said;
father will soon be here; the duke told me so with his own
lips. Oh, he is very good to me; he wants me to call him
father, and it is very strange; I feel as if he held my father's
place. I love him, too; but now I must call Lorenzo and
Gratiano, my dear companions; I am sure they must be on
the terrace together. Oh, that good Balthazar! I laugh at
his fun; hi, hi, hi! I am sure I can induce him to let me out
of the castle down into the camp, where my father will be
soon. Yes, I must bargain with him; we can all go without
being seen by anybody. Suppose the case that he should be
on guard at the postern during the next night. He will not
mind us. (*Gayly.*) Then I would shoot, gloriously, that
arrow over the battlements. (*Is about to shoot, when* BAL-
THAZAR *a jovial soldier, comes in.* (L. 1 E.)

BALTHAZAR. (*Pretending to ward off the arrow.*) Ho,
young milksop! these things must not be trifled with.

JUL. Dear Balthazar, I meant no harm—at least to you!
how glad I am to see you!

BAL. You are very good to say so, little one.

JUL. I can see no goodness in saying what I feel for you.

BAL. Julio, my boy, I am eternally obliged to you; but listen to me : this is no place to shoot.

JUL. I waited for you, Balthazar ; I thought you forgot our shooting exercise this morning. Were you not on the terrace with Gratiano and Lorenzo?

BAL. (*Seizing the arrow.*) No, boy; I was hurriedly despatched by Fabiano, our commander, to your father's camp below; there is news of an approaching battle. All is bustle and commotion. I ran back as fast as I could, and have been busy all the morning polishing my steel bow and other playthings. This toy of yours is good for practice, but would not do in a battle. (*Spiritedly.*) Give me my crossbow, and just hear the twang of its metal string; aha!

JUL. (*Afraid.*) Why, Balthazar, you chill me. I thought I was brave. Do soldiers use the crossbow with those sharp steel points?

BAL. Ay, lad; it gains ground every day, in spite of their laws and proclamations to keep up the yewen bow, because, forsooth, their grandsires shot with it, knowing no better. You see, Julio, war is no pastime; men will shoot at their enemies with the hittingest weapon and the killingest, not with the longest and the missingest.

JUL. Then these new engines I hear of will put both bows down; for these, with a pinch of black dust and a leaden ball and a child's finger, shall slay you Mars and Goliah and the Seven Champions.

BAL. Pooh, pooh! Petronel nor harquebus shall ever put down Sir Arbalest. Why, we can shoot ten times whilst they are putting their charcoal and their lead into their leathern smoke-belchers, and then kindling their matches. All that is too fumbling for the field of battle; there a soldier's weapons must be always ready, like his heart.

JUL. O Balthazar, I delight to hear you speaking to me in that way. I think that by your side I would fight like a lion!

BAL. You would swoon, I believe. No, I recant, Julio; you are a brave boy, but I cannot promise you that. Hush! some one is coming—Doctor Stephano, methinks, with his garrulous croaking. At your books, Julio; there, the thunderbolts are approaching; *au revoir.* (BALTHAZAR *rushes out on tiptoe by another passage,* R.U.E. LORENZO *and* GRA-TIANO *enter,* R. 2 E., *in a great hurry and with gay faces.*)

JUL. (*Attentive to his books, seems drawn from his studies by the arrival of his unexpected friends.*) Oh, what a surprise! Lorenzo! Gratiano! the noise you made frightened me. I thought it was old Stephano's light steps I heard sounding in the hall. (*Laughing.*) Well, what news?

LOR. Did you not hear what all the world knows?

GRAT. Well, Julio, we are simply surrounded by soldiers; the plain below is full of them, and more are coming.

JUL. Yes, Balthazar told me just now.

LOR. Balthazar! Was he with you? can it be possible that he has returned?

JUL. (*In low voice.*) Friends, do you wish to leave this place of confinement, and see the battle?

GRAT. To be sure. I am ready—I will fight too.

LOR. Oh, what sport! Do you think we can elude the vigilance of Stephano?

JUL. We can gain Balthazar over to us. Oh, I wish I could go there! My father will be engaged in the battle.

GRAT. Let's jump over the walls.

LOR. I can get a rope-ladder and place it on the walls, where it will reach the rock.

JUL. Yes, on the postern at the eastern wall.

GRAT. There is a guard there, watching all night, and you know sentinels have been doubled at all the posts.

JUL. Well, the best way is to go disguised with Balthazar. Wait, perhaps he has not left the next hall; I will bring him here. This must be decided now, this very hour. (*Exit,* R. U. E.)

LOR. We will wait impatiently; ho! some one is coming. Heavens! it is Stephano! (*Enter* STEPHANO, R. 2 E.)

STEPH. (*Coming, solemn and severe, with books under his arms.*) Ay, ay, I heard some noise in this room. What do I behold?—Lorenzo—Gratiano—here, and (*looks around*) where is Julio? Did you make this uproar alone?

GRAT. Good doctor, excuse us for the noise that you have heard; 'twas not meant to disturb your peace.

STEPH. Your hilarity I condemn. It is unbearable. Ah, young men, learn to be grave. (*They laugh.*) Withal, do not turn up your nose at my remarks. It is that grim, sturdy, middle-aged burgher Balthazar that blows the flame betwixt Julio and me, and sets you on. I have watched you, my lads, this while. Ay, you may stare.

LOR. Good doctor, we mean you no harm.

STEPH. Say no more; begone! begone!

BAL. (*Rushing in*, R.U.E., *with his bow.*) Oh! oh! the enemy will retreat with bag and baggage. (*Perceiving* STEPHANO.) Oh, 'twas an ambuscade! this old fox is not the ass he pretends to be. (*To* STEPHANO.) Oh, pardon, doctor! I fain would have recognized you in the full glory of your scientific mantle. I meant to pass without disturbing anyone. (*Goes out across the stage. Exit*, L. U. E.)

LOR. AND GRAT. Pardon, doctor, we will not disturb you any longer. (*Exeunt, mimicking him*, R. 1 E.)

STEPH. (*In passion.*) Young scapegraces, you will have your reward. (*Sees them gone.*) At last I may have peace and be alone while Julio is returning. My books - "*Dulce otium!*" Yes, my only friends, with you I have no war, no troubles: but, perhaps, I have been too hasty in rebuking those boys. Horace says that anger spoils everything, and Plato is not less positive in affirming that an ounce of choler is sufficient to poison a whole day's good. They are my scholars, and I owe to them an example as well as to Julio; but in such times as these in which we live everything is upset; no talk but of battles; nothing but a constant uproar and cries of alarm. (*Excited.*) They speak of a battle, of a siege, as if we were all going to be slain; reports are abroad that the fortress may be carried by assault. Then, what will become of me? The saying of the poet, "*Dulce bellum inexpertis*," does not apply to me; I see no fun in cracking the skulls of others, still less in having mine split. But where is Julio? Can it be that he forgets his class-hour? Julio is growing tall; his mind is fast maturing, and the tinkling of an armor brings fever to his brain; 'tis born with him, and all my sayings have been fruitless to divert his mind from the dangerous use of arms. He was not so four years ago, when his noble father sent for him a few days before that sad disaster of Arnoli, where he lost his chivalry in dreadful encounter with the Maceratans. Since that time the report of harquebuses pleases him, and my philosophy is at a discount. (*Cannon.* STEPHANO *jumps, frightened; soldiers rush in*, R. 2 E.)

LEONARDO. (*With his arms full of muskets.*) Quick, signor doctor! quick, scamper!—No soul idle here while there is a musket to fire. The enemy is on us, the battle has begun; up with us on the walls. (*Gives him a musket.*)

STEPH. Oh, Heavens! what can I do? I cannot fight; you know I never fought in my life.

LEON. No exception, no useless mouths here. The commander's orders, at the postern, every one.

STEPH. Oh, yes, here I go! (*Soldiers leave R. 2 E.*) Dear me! what can I do? (*He leaves, R.2E., hurriedly, handling awkwardly the gun.*)

SCENE II.

A Field. DUKE and RICCARDO discovered.

DUKE. This is the solemn moment, Riccardo, in which success may crown my arms, or reverse and destroy my hopes. The Prince of Macerata intends a bold stroke at us; it is evident that his forces are well equipped and numerous. Montefalco was not designed by him for a point of attack; ill-defended as it is, it could scarcely be esteemed by him worth the battle which will soon decide its fate. I see in this movement more than a desire to carry the fortress. I see the hand of Bartolo.

RICC. Bartolo, my lord! How could he know that this is Antonio's retreat?

DUKE. Beware, Riccardo! More than one traitor have I seen around me. Although the trusty men who have defended this castle for three years weave a sure network around Julio, yet I cannot forbear thinking that Bartolo has a clue to our most secret designs.

RICC. Then, my lord, may I receive your directions in case of a fatal turn of affairs? Suppose that the enemy succeed in driving our army from the walls?

DUKE. In this case—may God avert it!—here is a key, Riccardo; give it to Fabiano; it will open to him and Julio the door of the secret passage.

RICC. (*Receiving the key.*) I understand, my lord; but if he were killed in the combat, what then?

DUKE. I did not think of that, Riccardo. What we must defend, above all, is Julio. Let Fabiano remain by him and ward off danger from him. Entrust to Balthazar the command of the fortress; no better hands ever leveled the arbalest.

Mind my orders; let no enemy discover Julio. Adieu; I re-join my knights. (*Cannon are heard again.*) They press hard on us, I see; adieu; rejoin me promptly. (*He leaves hurriedly,* R. U. E.)

RICC. It is my prince's orders; I must obey. Strange events! Fortune, methinks, hovers above our heads; 'tis a mysterious eagle, now selecting a prey; justice claims its due. What I may do to protect Julio will avail little, I fear. But where is he? I must be away and have him taken out of danger. (*Exit,* R. 1 E.)

(*Enter* BALTHAZAR, L. 2 E.)

BAL. (*In bad humor.*) By the helmet of Mars, our pike-men are no better than a row of milksops! As for me (*bend-ing his cross-bow*), I'll die like a man, and the first coward of a renegado—. (*Seeing* LEONARDO *rushing in,* R. 2 E.) What is the matter now? (*A cannon is heard.*) Ah! they are men at last; well, if this is no cheat, there will be a trifle of a battle. Well, Leonardo, why do you stand here like an idiot? What news do you bring?

LEON. (*Scarcely able to speak.*) Julio is missing; we have searched all the fortress. Oh, what will our lord the duke say?

BAL. What is the matter now? Shall we tumble off our perch when we have nearly won the day? Why, man, you will frighten everyone. Julio cannot be out of the castle! Did you peep into his room? I'll go bail he is with that Nebuchadnezzar, Stephano.

LEON. (*Afraid.*) Stephano keeps aloof; no one has seen him the whole evening; some say that he has slipped into the well. (*Enter* MARSO, R. U. E.)

MARSO. (*To* BALTHAZAR, R.) Your honor, a rope-ladder hangs dangling from the wall at the postern; some treason, sir!

BAL. Aha! aha! this is a night fairly blowing. Get away, idiots! I know the mystery of that ladder; the young scamps did not wait for me to saunter off. Quick! follow me; Julio and the pages have made for the camp below. (*Exeunt.* L. U. E., *hastily.*)

(*Enter* STEPHANO *and* FABIANO, L. 1 E.)

STEPH. (*Peevishly.*) How could I help it, your honor? Could I watch him in the dark? Julio has been away from me the whole day.

Fab. My orders, sir, were that you should have your eyes on him all the time.

Steph. So have I done till this horrible day, sir.

Fab. Think not to excuse yourself, sir; you are responsible for any accident which may befal Julio. I was to receive him from you, in obedience to the duke's orders; and when I sent for you, you were found on the top of the tower. Is this doing your duty?

Steph. Indeed, sir, I will go to the end of the world to find him; he cannot be gone.

(*Enter* Leonardo, L.)

Fab. What news, Leonardo?

Leon. Julio has been found, your honor, down the rocks, ready to leap over the ditch. Loronzo and Gratiano were with him. Oh, sir, it is not Julio's fault.

Fab. Who arrested him, that I may reward him?

Leon. 'Twas Balthazar, your honor; he caught his crossbow and commanded them in the duke's name to stop or he would shoot them dead.

Fab. What! did he shoot them?

Steph. Oh, horrible! left them dead!

Leon. No. (*To* Stephano.) You are dead, you. (*To* Fabiano.) He did, your honor, but did them no harm; it scared them when they saw that he was in earnest. He shot ahead of them.

Step. Oh, good Heavens! here they come. (*Enter* Balthazar *with a* Soldier, *bringing in the boys*, L. U. E.)

Bal. 'Twas not too soon to give the alarm, my lord. The young scamps were nearly out of sight, but it is not their fault. If the watch had not been snoring away, they could never have crept out. May I ask you to forgive them?

Fab. The offence is too serious to be overlooked. Such foolish action in these present circumstances deserves an exemplary punishment.

Jul. Signor Fabiano, I ask that all the chastisement may fall upon me. It was I who plotted our escape.

Grat. It was I who fastened the rope.

Lor. I gave it, Signor Fabiano. I procured it; without me no escape was possible.

FAB.   And I summon you to tell me where you found the ladder.

STEPH.   (*Trembling.*)   It was I, my lord, it was I who had it. I had it concealed in my bed for my own use. When I went to to—to—use it, 'twas gone—gone!

BAL.   Oh! ah! old Aristotle, this is plausible for your worthy neck; you are the only cause of all the trouble.

FAB.   (*Aside.*)   Indeed, the whole affair turns out to be a farce.

BAL.   Your honor, command that the guilty be forthwith and peremptorily punished.

FAB.   Balthazar, I order that you take away Gratiano and Lorenzo, and lock them in the clock-tower with Stephano.

BAL.   The boys also, your honor?   The old fox gets clear cheap.   Come quick to your airy residence (*to* STEPHANO); it will take a long rope to slip from there, but you will have a fine view of our game below.   (*The boys and* STEPHANO, *with* BALTHAZAR, *leave*, R. U. E.)

FAB. (*To* JULIO.) Julio, it grieves me to see your rashness. You went against your father's orders, and I blame you for the whole affair.   Should the duke hear of it, you would incur his anger.

JUL.   My good Fabiano, forgive me—forgive my disobedience.   I see how much I have grieved you.   I alone am guilty; 'twas not Gratiano nor Lorenzo that led me; I did urge them on; I take all the blame on myself.   I wanted to see my father, and—   .

FAB.   Your candor disarms me, Julio.   I forgive you. (*Pressing him to his breast.*) You are frank in your confession.   I understand your desire of seeing your father, but you know it is now too late; the battle still rages; all that you can do is to pray that God may protect him.   Rest here during the night, and await the dawn of day in peaceful slumber. Adieu, Julio; I must be on the alert and send reinforcements to the duke.   (*Cannon heard.*)

JUL.   No sleep shall close my eyes while my heart is aching.   O my father! would that I might be with you in this dreadful hour! (*Cannon. Kneels*, c.) Merciful God, extend your protection over him and over the duke, and bring them safe to me.   (*Rises, sings. Music from the opera of "La Dame Blanche."*)

Oh, kind are the friends around me here,
  And gentle, and constant, and true:
But my father—my father so dear—
  There cannot be joy without you.
My father! oh, would thou wert here!

Then life would be sweet to my view.
  I sorrow, I sorrow, and mourn,
Lest my home I may never more see.
  Oh, why from my home was I torn?
Come, father, dear father, to me!

ACT THIRD.

SCENE I.

The Duke's room in the fortress of Montefalco Duke alone, eyes cast down, frowns, walks slowly.

DUKE. Thank Heaven, I am duke once more, with the brightest prospects before me! Spoleto reigns from sea to sea, except on that small speck of land on which stands Macerata. It was a bold engagement—yes, it was! My chances were few. His men, now slain and strewn on the plain by the hundred, were more brave than mine. *The right was with them, too.* Spoleto! thy bravery alone saved thee, for justice was not in thy ranks. The soldiers who followed me knew not my motives. Glory was *their* incentive; ambition was *mine!* This is why even in the midst of my triumph I do not feel at ease. To their eyes I am happy, but in my own I am wretched. Three years I have worked *that*— three years I have carried out a treacherous policy, and the edifice which I have built rests on the sand—on the discovery of Julio—Julio! (*Sadly.*) Yes! princely boy! He dreams not of my unjust dealings! He is all unconscious of what even a boy would regard as the greatest crime, unconscious of being stolen away from his father. Now Fortune smiles on me. I am sovereign of a vast domain. What shall I say to that boy? Shall I tell him that in the fight I met his father; that our lances were entangled, and that I threw him mercilessly on the ground; that I saw his eyes gleaming with fire and vengeance; that his venerable brow was besmeared with blood, and that his raven locks kissed the sod? Shall I reveal to him what my ears caught from his lips when he lay prostrate on the ground?—" Robber of my treasure, tell my Antonio that the thought of dishonor rends the heart of his

father more fiercely than that of death!" Shall I tell him
what he said when, abashed at the sight of my disarmed foe,
I rode away—those words which ring in my ear even now?—
"Go, bandit! God shall snatch thy prey from thee." (*Enter* STE-
PHANO, R.U.E.) Oh, this is what I heard, and in the very moment
of my dear triumph those words resound to my ears above the
shouts of victory. Yet the Fates bid me on. To delay would be
to increase the danger of Julio's discovery. To recoil would be
an injustice to my followers. I am forced to the deed; the
blood spilt urges me on. Would that at my last moments I
could reconcile my actions and my conscience! Would that
I could receive forgiveness from those I so cruelly wrong!
(*Perceives* STEPHANO.) Ah! here, Stephano? What
brings you here? (*Aside.*) Curse him if he heard me!

STEPH. My lord duke, I thought that something sad dis-
turbed your mind. I dared not come in sooner.

DUKE. You heard me, did you?

STEPH. I could hear little of what my lord said, it being
none of my business to listen to the sayings of your Excellency; but I thought I would usher myself into your presence
and, unobserved, bring to you this strange message. (*Gives
him an arrow with a letter attached.*)

DUKE. What can this mean? (*Reads the letter.*) You
read it, did you?

STEPH. I—*did*, your Excellency. It fell on the battlement
of the tower, and came whizzing by my face; Lorenzo, Gratiano and I read it.

DUKE. (*Quickly.*) Did Julio also read it?

STEPH. No, sir, only we three: we thought it might be
of importance—perhaps some treason—and—.

DUKE. Treason, no doubt, good Stephano. I understand
its meaning, but it is defeated by our victory—the traitor has
been slain. You may retire with our thanks, Stephano.

STEPH. Shall I keep it secret?

DUKE. It becomes your age to be discreet, and for aught
I know it is better not to make further mention of it. (*Exit*
STEPHANO, R. U. E.; *the* DUKE *flings the arrow outside.*)

DUKE. Zounds! this would confound the most resolute!
Double blunder! Fool that I was, to count with Bartolo!
This steel shaft was sent by one of his spies, no doubt. Why
did I not dispatch him when he was in my power? Can I

expect that he will now relent, and that he will value my momentary compassion on him, when I hold the dagger continually pointed at his heart? It is a lamentable fault to have mercy out of season! Victorious as I am, I little know the risk which even now I run. Speed and vigilance are more than ever necessary. I must see if Riccardo has returned from the pursuit. Perhaps he may have overtaken the Prince and Bartolo. Oh, it would be well! Riccardo is unscrupulous. It matters not to him on whom he raises his battle-axe. (*Enter* ANDREA, L. 2 E.)

ANDREA. Your Excellency, I come to announce the arrival of his honor, Riccardo; he desires an audience without delay: some important affair demands it, he says.

DUKE. Bring him in immediately. (*Exit* ANDREA, L. 2 E. *Returns with* RICCARDO, *and exit.*)

RICC. (*Bows.*) Lord duke, I come to make you aware of the result of our expedition. We arrived too late to prevent the enemy from entering Macerata.

DUKE. Your manœuvre was too slow.

RICC. Pardon, my lord. Rather say theirs was *too swift* for us, lord duke; they had the best horses; it was a close contest, though.

DUKE. Could you see them distinctly? You saw the prince and some of his courtiers: how many were they?

RICC. My lord, I saw the prince plainly; by his side rode a venerable warrior: both were dashing directly toward Macerata.

DUKE. (*Aside.*) It was Bartolo, I see—humph! (*Aloud.*) How many men had they?

RICC. I could not tell, as I little heeded their strength; my object was to head them and cut them off; yet from the noise of their horses' hoofs, I should think there were at least five hundred.

DUKE. Riccardo, speed to give our orders; everything must be ready for immediate departure; go, go! (*Exit* RICCARDO, L. 2 E.)

DUKE. Five hundred men! why did he not say five thousand, and at the same time tell me that Bartolo is no more? But he cannot escape. Macerata is a trap-hole where he shall be buried with his secret. Time is precious! I must see Fabiano. (*Musingly.*) He must by this time have informed Julio of the pretended death of his father. Fabiano

will tell him that Bartolo died bravely, fighting by my side,
and that his last words were of his Julio—that he begged the
duke to be his protector, his father. Ah, ah! All this looks
very plausible, if the air of sincerity beaming on good Fabiano's face is added to it, for Fabiano believes it himself, and,
forsooth, he feels the sad news deeply. Ah! here he comes.
(*Enter* FABIANO, R. I E.) Well, my good Fabiano, how did
Julio receive the cruel intelligence of his father's death?

FAB. I would rather fight two battles to one telling a boy
of his father's death, hard-hearted as I am.

DUKE. (*Hypocritically.*) It is a sad duty to perform,
Fabiano; 'tis enough to melt a heart of stone. Yet he knows
it? You told him all—that his father died at my side, that I
received his last words, and that he entrusted me with his beloved Julio?

FAB. I told him all I heard from your lips. I forgot nothing that would impress him; indeed, when I drew the picture
of that venerable knight, full of years and honor, dying only
a few paces from his son, and yet denied the pleasure of seeing him, I could not refrain from tears.

DUKE. I fain would weep myself. Did the thought that
I would accept him for my son soothe his sorrows? Do you
think he will soon forget that cruel bereavement?

FAB. Forget Bartolo! Oh, how could he? I myself
shall never forget this last interview with the boy; yet the
thought that there is one left to take a fatherly care of him
seemed to check his tears and moderate his grief; whilst there
is youth there is hope, and early grief is soon obliterated.

DUKE. Fabiano, receive my warm thanks for the sad duty
you performed in my stead. It would have grieved me beyond endurance to have told it to him myself. Receive again
my warm thanks, and prepare everything for a speedy departure. In the meantime bid the courtiers and my household
to meet in the great hall. Go! (*Exit* FABIANO, R.1E.) It matters
not to me when the secret is discovered, provided it remains
sealed two weeks longer. Macerata once mine, and the prince
disposed of, the people will be compelled to support me, whether
I have a son or not. (*Exit,* R. 2 E.)

SCENE II.

(LEONARDO *enters* R.1 E., *with bowed head, walking slowly.*)

LEON. Now, it puzzles me to know how this arrow came, and who shot it. I saw it rattling on the roof of the tower, but the knave kept aloof; the rogues have not all gone, I'll wager. What was that fellow doing on the rocks below, keeping his eyes on me as if he knew me? I'll warrant the rustic meant no good, strolling about the castle. Perhaps he himself sent that arrow : for when the stentorian voice of Stephano bellowed from the tower, the scamp cleared out through the narrow lane as if he saw sack and cord at his heels. (*Enter* STEPHANO, R.2 E.) Ah, bravo, Signor Stephano! it was you who drove the last enemy from our premises.

STEPH. (*With an air of importance.*) Perhaps I did, Master Leonardo. I was armed, too, and I would never swerve from my duty, sir—never! From the time I was a boy I always liked to chatter about battles and sieges. To hear the whizzing of arrows always woke me up, and the near approach of the enemy never failed to produce on me its wonted sensation. Oh, how often at night I have dreamed that I was engaged in the hottest of the fire, my helmet firm on my head and my body clad in complete armor, everybody shooting me!—archers shooting me !—cross-bow men shooting me!—and I never minding to be shot, so that at last I would get so demoralized as not to know when I was shot. I would walk the battlements on fire, as some stout skipper paces his deck in a suit of linsey-woolsey, calmly oblivious of the April drops that fall on his woolen armor. Yea, my besiegers would get spiteful, and would waste no more good steel on me, and I would laugh—ha, ha!

LEON. What avails it to be so brave in dreams, and hear your boasting when the battle is over, Signor Doctor?

STEPH. Hush, you unreasonable man! Do you think that I would seek the eye of the public, like that warlike vagabond, Balthazar, who would sling blazing tar-barrels if he could? God forbid!

LEON. Disguise it as you will, sir, bravery is bravery, and this is what rid us of our enemies last night.

STEPH. Idle chat! idle chat! When you have slain all your enemies, and in the end lie a helpless corpse yourself, is your country the better for that? Are you the better yourself? Was not Greece saved by the retreat of the Ten Thousand? Their retreat, sir, was commendable, and worthy of the admiration of all ages.

LEON. And it was out of admiration for those Greeks that you hobbled to the tower's top in such a great hurry?—ha! ha!

STEPH. Ay! you call that hobbling? (*Peevishly.*) It was a narrow escape for you as well as for me. For if the fellow had reached the loophole,—it chills my blood in my veins to think of it! But I kicked down the ladder, and the vagabond nearly broke his skull. Ay, sir, we all ran the greatest risk; I was at a loss for a minute whether to fly and hide myself, and let the place be taken by the ruffians, or, sir, to defend my post at the cost of my life, and play havoc among them: and this, with the help of God, I have done, for I spread panic in their ranks;—ay, and to increase their terror, I nodded at them, sir, and grinned at them; then, in defiance, I roared out at them, "*Videamus quamdiu audebitis in hac aula morari.*" They shook like aspens, and stole away on tiptoe—one by one at first, then in a rush—and left me alone. Then I lost all consciousness, and the next thing I can well remember is my waking up in the tower when Signor Fabiano sent you after me.

LEON. (*Wondering, aside.*) Ro-co-la, ra-ri! Pouah! These are the words I heard you mumbling, with your mouth wide open and your body all in a sweat. Such a gibberish! It was a terrible nightmare, sir— ha!

STEPH. I never saw the like of it in Cæsar or Xenophon.

BAL. (*Entering, eying old* STEPHANO.) Ah! ah! old Beelzebub, it was your croaking that spoiled my shot and scared the game away. I would have stripped him of his doublet and jerkin, but your irreverent howling made him prance away, and so it went wide of him two inches. By Hannibal's helmet, I thought I would make another gap in the roof of the tower and make you converse with him by signs, but my respect for property, and the fear of hitting my milksops, nestling with you, prevented my doing it. Zounds!

STEPH. It would be little worthy of you, and it would make you none the braver to kill an old man after the battle is over. For my life I would give little. The arrow did not hurt me, although it might as well, to please you.

BAL. What, then! did it harm the boys?

STEPH. I dared not give the alarm to the duke, but Lorenzo was badly touched: I attended to him; he will soon do well.

BAL. In truth, you are no peevish child, Stephano. I thought you were all skins and parchments, and I used you wrong, but now I confess I have been a boorish archer. Here's my hand, Stephano. Come to see the boys. Poor things! I must see that nothing is amiss with them. (*To* LEONARDO.) And you, popinjay, it is no time to look awry: go and pack up your traps. (BALTHAZAR *starts to go*, R., *but* STEPHANO *detains him.*)

STEPH. (R., *looking to see if* LEONARDO *is gone.*) Balthazar, I have something on my mind to tell you.

BAL. Ay, to me: anything you please, Stephano; you have done me a good turn in tending that boy's wound. I am all ears to you. Why do you stare so strangely with your ashy face?

STEPH. (*Confidentially.*) On the arrow there was a letter.

BAL. Humph, a letter! and what was in that letter? Did you keep it?

STEPH. No, I would not cut my throat for what does not concern me; I took it to the duke.

BAL. What! Did you not read it?

STEPH. I did.

BAL. What did it say?

STEPH. It read in this way: "Antonio, I know that you are here; I will do all in my power to see you.—BARTOLO."

BAL. Some foolery, I will wager. And the duke laughed in your face, did he?

STEPH. No, he seemed very serious. It was a treason, he said.

BAL. Oh, bah! By Jupiter, it was the knave who sent that arrow. No matter, I will think of it, Stephano; I will see if some time I can splice that on to something else. By the way, did you not mark how sad Julio looked to-day? I will venture to say the duke was informed, by some one, of his escapade. The wretch who did it deserves to be trounced.

STEPH. It was not I, Balthazar; I would not grieve Julio's heart for the whole of Montefalco.

BAL. I know you well now, Stephano. Come, I will see what is the matter; come, everybody must be in the hall now. (*Exeunt*, R. I E.)

SCENE III.

The great hall—DUKE on a throne with JULIO. All the courtiers surrounding the throne—BALTHAZAR (R.), STEPHANO (L.), the farthest from the throne.

DUKE. Nobles, and you of my household, be attentive to what I have to make known to you, and to all my people, whom you now represent. You all know the sad events which have marked the three years of disturbance and bloodshed brought upon us by unjust aggression from one nearly related to me. You know his aim— with what a covetous eye he beheld our fertile lands and our prosperous towns. My efforts to elude his designs need not to be recalled. What you have done to assist and support me extorts my unfeigned acknowledgments and gratitude. With me you rejoice in our glorious achievements, the fruit of which you shall enjoy. Yet, even in the midst of our exultation, even after the decisive triumph of yesterday, one thought weighs on my mind—one fear which I endeavor in vain to shake off, and yet the realization of which might be the source of new disasters and irreparable ruin to our enterprise,—I fear I shall die before I succeed in the overthrow of my enemy.

ALL. God forbid, good duke !

DUKE. I am mortal : death may strike me at any hour ; but I have provided for what may come, and therefore, according to the custom of my ancestors and to the laws of our country, I name my successor. Should I die in this struggle, behold my only, my legitimate heir in my son Julio.

ALL. Long life to our worthy lord duke and his son Julio!

RICC. Long life to the legitimate heir of Spoleto! (*They bring a crown to* JULIO. *The* DUKE *places it on his head.*)

BAL. And soon of Macerata! I will venture that I shall yet bring him in.

STEPH. Tush, tush, Balthazar ! you're always boasting.

DUKE. My lords, do you promise obedience ? Do you pledge yourselves to serve the interest of my heir and successor ?

ALL. (*Raising their hands.*) We pledge ourselves to serve him, and may God help us !

DUKE. Then, let it be heralded throughout our dominions.

Let our loyal subjects rejoice and the foe tremble in his last retreat, for now we will march on Macerata and there plant our banners.

JUL. My lord duke and much honored father, permit me to acknowledge the marks of kindness you have shown toward me, especially this last and least expected; and also, allow me, before you depart for new scenes of danger, to ask to follow you, with my companions Lorenzo and Gratiano. For three years I have not quitted these walls, and scarcely know the meaning of the great dignity you have just conferred on me. I also desire to win fame and renown, and render myself worthy to command.

DUKE. And you would wish to share our dangers and our glory before Macerata? My son, an accident might happen to you; you are yet inexpert.

ALL. We will protect him—we will defend him!

DUKE. And which of you will pledge his life for Julio's?

BAL. I will. I'll pledge it ten times over.

JUL. My lord duke, Balthazar has been ever faithful to me. It is to him that I owe my knowledge in archery. With him I feel secure.

DUKE. Let your wishes be gratified. Balthazar, you answer for Julio, on your life; mind my word!

BAL. I shall, my lord! Zounds! What is he thinking about! There is no danger where I am.

DUKE. And now let us depart. Riccardo, you shall lead the van of the army. I will command the centre, and Fabiano shall bring up the rear and see to the baggage-trains and supplies.

FAB. Your Excellency, everything is in readiness.

DUKE. Forward, then; all, on to Macerata.

ALL. Macerata! Macerata!

STEPH. (*Aside to* BALTHAZAR.) Did you notice how sad Julio looked?

BAL. I did. Bull of Bashan! something goes wrong. I shall soon know it. (*Exeunt*, R. 2 & 3 E., *all in solemn order. Martial music.*)

ACT FOURTH.

SCENE I.—The Besieged Town.

Interior of a large church, where armed men are congregated, all in
kneeling attitude. In the centre of the farthest end of the church is
BARTOLO, also kneeling, half turned away from the front of the stage.
A solemn chant is heard, and when it has died away, in the midst of
the greatest silence BARTOLO rises, advances, and addresses the kneeling assembly.

BARTOLO. Friends, and my companions, we have just in-
voked the last blessing of God on our well-nigh ruined hopes.
This is the most solemn moment of our lives, because, prob-
ably, the last given to us to breathe freely before the foe shall
load our hands and feet with chains, and cast us into gloomy
dungeons. God avert, my friends, this degradation from us,
who for three years have fought in defence of our sacred
rights! It is true, we have lost everything. We are now
reduced to the defence of the last remnant of Macerata's
power. It must be upheld at any cost. It must never be
said that we have faltered at the supreme hour. Let not the
enemy pride himself on his conquest, and boast that he will
reap the cost of his labors. Would that I could be heard by
every Maceratan at this solemn moment! would that I could
inspire with my own sentiments those who talk of terms and
surrender! I would say to them: You have lost everything
 your prestige is gone, your glory is of the past, your goods
are to be the booty of the victor. Why should you preserve
them for him? Why lower yourself to become beggars of
the Spoletan in your own princely town? Destroy it; let not
one stone remain upon another, and out of every ruin let a
rampart be made, and defy the foe!

(*Enter* PIETRO, L. 2 E.)

PIETRO. My commander, a deputation of the citizens of
the town desire to be introduced.

A FEW. Yes, let them come; they have something to say
in the matter.

(*Enter* ALBERTO, GABRINI, CASTELLO *and* ORAZZI, L. 2 E.
They bow respectfully.)

ALBERTO. Count Bartolo, we beg to submit to you our
wishes, and those of the people.

BART. Are you sure you speak in the name of the people? What do the people say?

ALB. They are reduced to their last morsel. They can stand it no longer.

BART. And they speak of surrender?

ALB. Or whatever you say. It is for you to decide in the name of the prince.

BART. Well, listen to me, and carry them my answer. I, Bartolo, in the name of the prince of Macerata, my sovereign and yours —I bid you summon the people and tell them that we will try one last effort to drive back the enemy. Tell them to flock to the standard of the prince, who is now on the walls preparing for a sortie. Should they hesitate, tell them that I, who have lost everything in your defence—I, who mourn even my own son's murder at the hands of the barbarous foe with whom they intend to treat,—tell them that I shall never surrender, and woe to the Spoletans whom I shall meet! Woe to the duke, should I meet him in battle! And God forbid! He, too, has a son. May he never fall into Bartolo's hands!

ALL. Bravo, bravo! Bartolo, we will stand by you.

ALB. Rely on us, Count Bartolo; we shall do our duty, and all the people of Macerata with us. We prefer to die rather than surrender!

BART. (*To* CITIZENS.) Go forth, then, and tell the people that the enemy is now pressing the forces of the prince at the western gate (*exeunt*); and you, my companions, go to your commands, and rouse your men to do their duty. (*Exeunt,* L. 2 E. *As* BARTOLO *is about to leave,* GIACOMO *rushes in* L. 1 E.)

GIAC. Bartolo, my noble master! Everything is against us; the prince has just fallen, pierced to the heart by an arrow. He expired in my arms.

BART. (*Falling on his knees.*) O God, have mercy on the remnant of a faithful people! Let Thy anger be appeased by this cruel blow. (*Rises.*) Giacomo, on me now devolves the first command. Go! bid all the forces yet disposable to fly to the rescue where the prince has fallen, and sustain the shock of the enemy. They will, I fear, take advantage of the loss and overpower our forces. Go with all speed. (*Exit* GIACOMO; *enter* SILVIO, L. 2 E.)

SILVIO. My lord, good news! the enemy is beaten back with heavy loss. Our men have followed them into their very

entrenchments, and many prisoners are secured. The duke's
son is among them, and the people would have torn him in
pieces but for a tall soldier who was captured with him.

BART. The duke's son in our hands! Zounds! This is a
just retribution. Oh, it is not too late for vengeance! Hurry
back, and tell the people that whoever touches the boy shall
answer for the least injury done to him with his own life. By
all means let him be preserved for the ransom of the town.
Now we can treat with the proud Spoletan; we shall see if he
will defy us now. Go—quick! Wait! let the two prisoners
be thrown into the dungeon of the fortress; give my orders.

SIL. I will do so at once. (*Exit*, R. 2 E.)

BART. If I had my choice between the duke's defeat and
death, and this chance of revenge, I think I would choose the
latter. For years I have waited to avenge the injury done to
me. For years I have sought my Antonio, until I knew for
certain that he was no more. But now in exchange I have
his son—his only son, too. It is well that there is justice in
heaven. But let me forget my own thirst for vengeance, and
see if the duke will come to terms. (*He writes.*) Here is
my message to him: "Duke of Spoleto, the chances of war
have placed thy son in my hands; be not rash, but consider
my proposition: thou shalt forthwith abandon the siege of
Macerata, and retire from the lands of the prince. In case
thou dost not immediately conform to our terms, thy son shall
forfeit his life.—BARTOLO." Ho, here! (*Enter* PACIFICO, R. 2 E.)
Go with this message to the walls, and hoist the flag of truce;
this is important; it must reach the duke immediately; go!
(*Exeunt* BARTOLO, L. 2 E., *and* PACIFICO, R. 2 E.)

SCENE II.--PRISON.

BALTHAZAR and JULIO are brought in, R. 2 E., followed by the Jailer with
keys, and a Blacksmith with chains.

JAIL. Here, you grizzly Ganymede, and you, my lamb,
here's your lodging for the present.

BAL. The fellow must be well patronized to keep such
rooms in his house! Curse them for getting me into this trap!

JUL. Balthazar, do not irritate him; he might do us more
harm.

BAL. Tush, you boy! Is this a place for civil people to
be quartered? Zounds! I have a mind to thump the fellows
and crawl out.

JAIL. What do you say? Oh, be not afraid, we will not let you stay here. (*Going away.*) Zucchi, do your duty; that will quell him a little. (*Exit*, R. 2 E.)

BAL. Imbecile that I have been! Zounds! if I can give him his pay sometime!

ZUC. Hallo, my fine fellows! It is not so bad after all; many a poor wretch gets worse than this, and but for that little urchin you might be now swinging from the top of the tower. Well, it is not my fault. One must live, and if you give me a trifle I will not riddle your skin too bad.

JUL. Cruel man! So you imagine that we need your pincer's work on us!

ZUC. It is the order, my lamb. Do you see I am paid for the trouble, and faith it is not too much for us poor people to bleed you a little.

BAL. Look here, man! will you desist from fastening the tender boy's limbs? I will give you double pay.

ZUC. Think he would swoon, eh? Hi, hi, hi!

BAL. For shame! The man has no heart that we can reach. Go on; do your work; I will pay for two, but I will get my money back, I promise you!

ZUC. (*Fastening the irons on* BALTHAZAR's *feet.*) By Jupiter! it is not every man's shoes that you could wear—hem!

JUL. Man, my father will reward you if you are kind to us.

ZUC. I know that voice! Sure as I live, I have heard it before. It sounds like Antonio's voice.

BAL. Why do you not go on? The sooner you dispatch us the better.

ZUC. That will come soon enough, as we have no bread to waste; but tell me, man, is this the duke's son?

BAL. Guess: you are an old fox as well as a wolf.

ZUC. (*Working.*) Does not hurt you, eh?

BAL. I am much obliged to you, sir—quite comfortable.

ZUC. Now, your turn, boy. What is your age?

JUL. Seventeen, sir.

BAL. Julio, I command you to hold your tongue. Indeed, the fellow wants to question us a little more than I am in humor to bear. Sir, fastened as I am, I can give you some trouble yet; therefore, mind to do your work in quick time.

Zuc.   Hallo, sir, you speak like a book!

Bal.   Like one who cares little where he leaves his bones.

Jul.   Ah, ah, sir, you hurt me horribly!

Zuc.   'Tis nothing—nothing at all.   You see, your foot is too small; I have to press your ankles a little. (*Rises.*)

Bal.   Be firm, Julio; do not wince, boy.   I have shot enough of these vultures to pay for it now.   Zounds! that last gay jerkin I laid low was no hare, forsooth!   I was no bungler that time, but I was a fool to stare at his struggling for sweet life.   I was a fool to tear my silk scarf and bind his wounds, as if he had been my brother, but it shook me to see a fellow-creature so discomforted.   It made my heart ache.   Then I was gobbled up by those heartless knaves.

Zuc.   And for it you will be greeted by the next tree, Sir Crossbow-man, for the gay jerkin was the Prince of Macerata himself.   This is worth a purse full of gold to me.   Goodbye; I will meet you again.   (*Exit,* L. 2 E.)

Jul.   (*Nearly fainting, falling on* BALTHAZAR's *arms.*) Balthazar, I am horribly tortured; I feel as if I were dying; all my bones ache.   Balthazar, when shall we leave this dreary prison?

Bal.   (*On one knee, and resting* JULIO *on the other.*) Now I am undone!   Curse them!   I had sworn that neither want nor harm should come to him, and now to have him confined in this confounded hole!

Jul.   (*In lower voice.*)   Balthazar, I have something on my mind to tell you, as we are alone.

Bal.   (*Aside.*)   I fear he is delirious.

Jul.   (*Speaking slowly.*)   Balthazar, you have been deceived concerning me; my name is not Julio; I am not the son of the duke.

Bal.   Now he is crazed.   Oh, those vultures!

Jul.   My name is Antonio, and my father's name was Bartolo; ay, ay!   The duke took me from my father when I was much younger, and brought me up as his son Julio, whom I resembled, he said.   My father was killed near Montefalco, so the duke told me: and now, O Balthazar, I have said all, I am ready to die.

Bal.   Good Heavens! what story is this?   The boy seems to have his senses, and tell the truth.   Oh, I remember the arrow and the letter now.   As I live, Antonio and Bartolo were mentioned there. But it was after the battle. Bartolo cannot be dead, then. I am puzzled. Ah, some one is coming, Julio; wake up, stand up, Julio; they come for us. (*Enter* JAILER, R. 2 E.)

JAIL. (*Abruptly.*) Now, my pets, your turn is coming; it will not be long. (*Enter* ORLANDO, R. 1 E.)

ORLANDO. (*To the* JAILER.) Sir, I command here! You have not a word to say to these prisoners. Sir Cross-bowman, you are accused of the prince's murder; you will therefore accompany the son of the Duke of Spoleto, and with him receive your sentence from the commander himself.

BAL. Well, this one is a polite cut-throat! Ready, sir: come, Julio, let me help you, poor lamb!

JUL. Balthazar, let me pass my arm around you. Now I can walk. (*They go off*, R. 2 E., *slowly, dragging the irons.*)

SCENE III. TENT OF THE DUKE.

DUKE. (*After writing an order.*) It is strange I feel as I do. I believe it is the first time in my life that I have ever doubted of success when success was within my reach. (*Walks excitedly.*) Fool that I am! can I not shake off these impressions? Perhaps too much success has accustomed me so little to the idea of opposition that the mere thought is a heavy weight on my soul. (*Thoughtfully.*) The only reverse which may befall me is in the resistance of the Maceratans. True, their town can stand a long siege; they are resolute, and they have expert leaders. But what of that? I will starve them out, and bar all access to supplies. We shall then see if our good prince will not come to terms. Terms! no; I shall accept no terms. He must perish. Better for him to perish sword in hand, and spare me the necessity of staining my glory with his blood. Bartolo, too, must perish! He above all! Bartolo, my most dangerous foe, must be quickly disposed of. I could bear to see the prince a fugitive through the land; but Bartolo is a spy, an accuser, an avenger, wherever he is. Let me see: suppose I send in a proposition —yes, ha, ha, ha!—a hand-to-hand combat with him, on the result of which shall depend my withdrawal from the town or its surrender. I will send the proposition to the prince; perhaps he will accept. (*He writes.*) "I, duke of Spoleto, pledge myself—" (*Enter* RICCARDO, L. 1 E., *in haste.*)

Ricc.   My lord, my lord, I am the bearer of good news;
the prince has just been killed outside of the ramparts; his
body is in our hands.

Duke.   Thanks to Heaven!   Riccardo, you shall have
your reward for such good news.   How are our prospects of
success?

Ricc.   Fair, indeed; another day and the town shall be
ours.

Duke.   Riccardo, go back; bring me the news of Bartolo's
death, and the principality of Macerata is yours.   Despatch is
necessary, for the enemy will no doubt deal us a heavy blow
to avenge their loss.

Ricc.   I go, my lord; remember your promise. (*Exit*, L. 1 E.)

Duke.   A promise is a good stimulant, I fancy.   But what
do I see?   Our men are driven back; the foe is on us.   (FA-
BIANO *rushes in*, L. 2 E.)

Fab.   My lord, we need reinforcements immediately; we
are losing ground.   They have driven our forces two hundred yards from the walls, and recaptured the prince's body.

Duke.   What do you say?   Are you mad, Fabiano?   Are
not Balthazar and his crossbow-men at their work?

Fab.   I have just lost sight of him in the mêlée.   But he
lacks men, my lord.   The enemy is driven to desperation.

Duke.   *You* are driven to desperation.   What!   Fly before a handful of men!   Shame, for shame!

Leon.   (*Rushing in*, L. 2 E., *breathless.*)   My lord—.

Duke.   What ominous news does he bring?

Leon.   Horrible!   Ju—Julio is—captured.

Duke.   What! captured?—Julio?   Are you mad?

Leon.   True, as I say, my lord; Julio is captured, and
Balthazar too!

Duke.   Desperation!   All to the rescue!   follow me!
(*Exeunt all*, L. 3 E., *except* LEONARDO.)

Leon.   (*Raising up his hands, astounded.*)   San Petruc-
chio! what a misfortune!

Steph.   (*Entering*, R. 1 E., *amazed.*)   What is to be done?
Have you all gone crazy in this awful uproar?   Where are
they all going?

Leon.   Going!   Why, man, I thought you were captured!
Do I behold Stephano?

STEPH. (*Looking at himself.*) To be sure! what else could I be?

LEON. A corpse, sir.

STEPH. A corpse! And why so, sir? (*Aside.*) The man's mind is gone, surely. (*Looks out in the direction of the city*, L.) But see the duke. Ay! hearken to the trumpets!

LEON. (*Sneering.*) Hearken to the trumpets, do you not? Some one must have unearthed you this moment, for the trumpet's blast is deafening us the last three days. (*Looks toward the city.*) But see the duke on his gray charger, springing on the foe!

STEPH. Good Heavens! what rashness! Did you ever see? (*Sees* RICCARDO *brought in wounded*, L.) Oh, horror! my lord Riccardo wounded!

RICC. Lay me here, men, and go back to protect the duke, The day is won! Go, go!

LEON. (*Looking sadly on* RICCARDO.) Can I assist you, my lord?

RICC. All help is useless. Do not stay idling around me. Go to the ramparts; there work is in plenty. Julio is not rescued yet

STEPH. (*Astounded.*) What! Julio not rescued! What does he mean?

LEON. (*Forcibly.*) He means that when you were dreaming in some corner of the camp, Julio was captured while he was fighting bravely at Balthazar's side. Cowardly old pedagogue!

STEPH. (*Oppressed with emotion.*) Julio, my poor boy, is captured? Oh, let me go—what can I do to save him?

LEON. (*Taking off his sword.*) Here is a sword, man. There, you see the enemy; there are the walls. You must kill the first and storm the others!

STEPH. *I must!* you say. Yes, I may as well die now. (*Exit* STEPHANO, L. 3 E., *hurriedly.*)

LEON. (*Sees him gone.*) Indeed he is gone! Poor man! What can he do for Julio, except to share his fate? (*Looking at* RICCARDO.) My lord! (*No answer.*) My lord! Alas! he too is dead. (*Takes* RICCARDO's *sword.*) It would be cowardice not to avenge so many misfortunes. I swear I will not be the last in the breach. (*Exit*, L. 3 E.)

(*Enter* PACIFICO, R. 2 E., *the messenger of* BARTOLO.)

PACIFICO. (*Looking on.*) What do I behold? Is not this the ducal escutcheon? Yes—*deserted!* (*Sees* RICCARDO.) No! a dead man here. Unfortunate! thy hour, too, has come. But the duke, where is he? (*Aloud.*) Ho! some one here! No one comes. Here I will leave my message. (*Goes to place it on a table, and finds there the letter of the* DUKE *to* BARTOLO.) What is this? (*Reads.*) "I, Duke of Spoleto, pledge myself to retire from the walls of Macerata, in case of the fatal issue of the single combat to which I challenge Bartolo," etc. No doubt it was intended to be sent to its destination. Joyously will I carry it, duke of Spoleto; for, thanks to Heaven, it will be thy doom. (*Exit*, L. 2 E.)

SCENE IV.—HALL OF JUSTICE.

BARTOLO and a few Guards.

BART. (*To the guards.*) Guards, watch with eager eye the advance of the enemy, for he must not overtake us, whilst we may yet do him harm and deal him the last blow which a merciless justice has placed in our power. (*To the warriors.*) That we have lost all is well known to you, brave men; we now but wait the doom which, few as we are, we cannot expect to elude. I have done all in my power to dictate terms which I thought the duke would accept. The threatened death of his son, in case he should not comply with our just desires, has had no effect. Let him, therefore, take all responsibility on himself alone for what I have pledged myself to do. And when, sword in hand, he shall enter this hall, let the lifeless body of his boy greet him. Then he will know what it has cost him to gain a ruined city, now reeking with the blood of its murdered inhabitants.

ALL. It is but justice. Let it have its course.

BART. Guards, bring in the prisoners.

(*Enter* BALTHAZAR, *preceded by an officer, followed by two men*, L. 2 E. BALTHAZAR *conceals the boy from* BARTOLO *by placing himself in front of him.*)

BAL. Come, Julio! I have shown you how to behave in battle—I will show you how to die.

JUL. I am not afraid, friend.

BART. Whose voice is that? (*Steps forward.*) Whom do I see? Heaven, have pity on me, it is my Antonio! (*Rushes towards* JULIO.)

BAL. (*Keeping him back.*) Avaunt, man! (JULIO be-
holds BARTOLO *and recognizes him.*)

JUL. Ah! my father! (*Rushes to his father; they fall
into each other's embrace, and remain clasped.*)

ALL. His father! It is his son!

BART. (*Looking at* JULIO.) Is this a dream? Is it you,
my Antonio? (*Standing erect, one arm around* JULIO, *his
sword drawn; with defiant mein he looks at his men, who,
all with drawn swords, cluster around.*) Good God! I thank
Thee!

BAL. What must I believe? Antonio—Bartolo! strike
off my chains—I understand all now! Give me a sword!

BART. (*Sadly.*) It is late. It is sad to be happy, and
yet to have to part. It is better, perhaps.

BAL. Woe to the one who shall first show his face to me,
I will swear! Bartolo, I will strike for thee!

(*Enter, from back of stage, the* DUKE *and a host of others,
hurriedly, sword in hand.*)

DUKE. (*Pointing out* JULIO *to his men.*) Save him!
(*To* BALTHAZAR.) Ah! traitor!

BAL. Never! Back, duke of Spoleto! (*Presses upon
him with his sword; they fight; all look on this strange
spectacle;* JULIO *is in his father's arms horrified.*)

DUKE. (*Falls, c.*) Oh, spare me! Have pity on me!

BAL. (*Looking on the prostrate form.*) Wretched man!
Justice has at last overtaken you!

DUKE. Bartolo, it is just; forgive my wrongs to thee! I
claim thy pardon. Bartolo! Julio!

BART. Wretched man, I forgive you! Yes, here is my
hand.

ALL. This is indeed a mystery!

BAL. It is a mystery of theft and murder.

DUKE. It is ambition and ruin! Woe to me, for I have
trifled with a father's love and with the blood of thousands!

BART. Duke of Spoleto, die in peace; I forgive you:
Antonio forgives you.

JUL. Ah! yes, with all my heart I forgive you. A child's
forgiveness rest lovingly on you!

DUKE. God bless you, boy! Let all remember that you

are my heir, and love you as I did. Ah, mercy of God, I now sigh for thee. I die; good God, pity—mercy!

JUL. (*Coming to him and lovingly raising his head.*) We all forgive you, my lord.

DUKE. God bless you, Julio! (*He expires; all remain in silence.*)

JUL. He is dead!

BAL. But you live, boy, a duke and a prince; it is enough.

JUL. Say a king, for now I have my father!

ALL. Long life to our duke!

MACERATANS. Long life to our prince!

BART. Let us return thanks to God, and may peace now reign supreme!

TABLEAU.

SLOW, PLAINTIVE MUSIC.

EPILOGUE.

Of self-deceit, the folly grave
Is seen, in contrast with the brave,
Straightforward truth of open dealings,
Which feels, yet weighs, another's feelings.
Had envious Spoleto given
Less thought to earth and more to Heaven,
Bartolo's fond, paternal heart
Had felt not the keen, cruel dart
Of grief at fair Antonio's loss;
From his broad dukedom, many a loss
Had been averted. But we see
That crime from justice may not flee:
Happy, if it come not too late.
Ah! if till death it shall await.
Who, who, can tell its rigors there,
Beyond the reach of hope, of prayer!
But with delight the course we follow
Of wronged and yet redressed Bartolo:
And thanking all our good friends present
For lenient judgment, smiles so pleasant.
We fondly trust that each one's years,
With change, successes, hopes and fears,
Will turn out in as good condition
As Julio's in "THE RECOGNITION!"

NEW BOOKS.

——o——

A TROUBLED HEART, AND HOW IT WAS COMFORTED AT LAST. Price, $1.50

JOSEPH HAYDN—THE STORY OF HIS LIFE, translated from the German of Franz von Seeburg, by the Rev. J. M. Toohey, C. S. C., Vice President of the University of Notre Dame, Ind. 350 pp. Price, $1.50

THE AMERICAN ELOCUTIONIST AND DRAMATIC READER, for the use of Colleges, Academies, and Schools. Contains the celebrated Drama, "The Recognition." 468 pp. Price, $1.50

THE HOUSEHOLD LIBRARY OF CATHOLIC POETS, from Chaucer to the present day. The only work of its kind in the language. Subscription Edition (with an admirable portrait of Chaucer). Price, $5.00 Cheap Edition. $2.00

THE SCHOLASTIC ANNUAL for 1885. Tenth Year. Price, 25c

OTHER BOOKS IN PREPARATION.

NEW PLAYS.

FOR MALE CHARACTERS ONLY.

THE MALEDICTION. A Drama in Three Acts. Translated and adapted from the French. Price, 50c

IF I WERE A KING. A Drama in Four Acts. Price, 50c

LE BOURGEOIS GENTILHOMME; or THE UPSTART. A Comedy in Three Acts. Adapted from the French of Moliere. Price, 25c

ROGUERIES OF SCAPIN. A Comedy. Translated from the French. Price, 25c

THE PRODIGAL LAW STUDENT. A Drama in Four Acts. Price, 50c

THE EXPIATION. A Drama in Four Acts. [Only a very few copies on hand.] Price, 50c

THE RECOGNITION. A Drama in Four Acts, of the Fifteenth Century. Price, 50c

OTHER DRAMAS IN COURSE OF PREPARATION.

Any of the above publications sent free of postage on receipt of retail price. A liberal discount to dealers and those purchasing in quantities. Address,

Prof. J. A. LYONS, Notre Dame, Ind.

www.ingramcontent.com/pod-product-compliance
Lightning Source LLC
Chambersburg PA
CBHW030905260626
47169CB00008B/2700